Don't be a bully, Billy

A Cautionary Tale

Phil Roxbee Cox

Illustrated by Jan McCafferty

Edited by Jenny Tyler

De _____ igg

First published in 2004 by Usborne Publishing Ltd., 83-85 Saffron Hill, London, EC1N 8RT www.usborne.com
Copyright © 2004 Usborne Publishing Limited. The name Usborne and the devices ♀ ⊕ are Trade Marks of Usborne Publishing Ltd.
First published in America in 2004. UE. Printed in Dubai.

Meet Billy.

Billy is a bully.

Every day at school,

Billy punches...

Billy snatches...

Billy pulls...

and Billy scratches...

...and everyone begs,

"Don't be a bully, Billy!"

But Billy keeps on bullying.

Billy the bully kicked Kevin...

...and kicked Kevin cried,

"Don't be a bully, Billy!"

and rubbed his knee.

Billy the bully shook Shaun...

...and shaken Shaun shouted,

"Don't be a b-b-bully, Billy!"

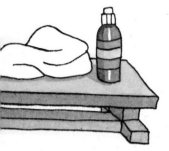

and tried to stop sh-sh-shaking.

Billy the bully picked on Paula...

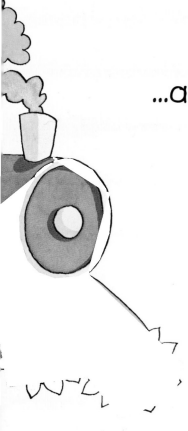

...and picked-on Paula pleaded,

"Don't be a bully, Billy!"

and wiped away her tears.

Billy the bully chased Charlie...

12

...and chased Charlie panted,

"Don't be a bully, Billy!"

and hid around the corner.

13

It's Monday morning.
Billy the bully is
threatening Theo.

Then, on the way to class, he barges into Belinda...

At lunchtime, Billy the bully
pushes Peter into his pudding...

16

...so threatened Theo,
barged-into Belinda and
pudding-plastered Peter plead,

"Don't be a bully, Billy!"

But Billy keeps on bullying.

After school, Billy follows Bob, the new boy, on his way home.

He's all by himself.

18

Billy snatches Bob's ball, and Bob says,

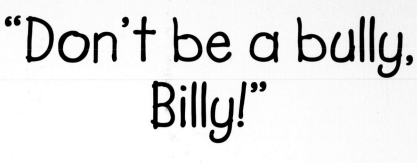

"Don't be a bully, Billy!"

"Give it back, it's mine!"

"Make me!"
says Billy the bully.

"I don't have to," says Bob.

"Meet my **Big Brother.**" Bob points up to the sky.

"Hi!" says Bob's big brother.
"You're coming for a ride!"

"HELLLLP!"
hollers helpless Billy...

23

But Billy's bullied
schoolmates simply shout,
"Bye-bye, Billy!"

and happily head for home.